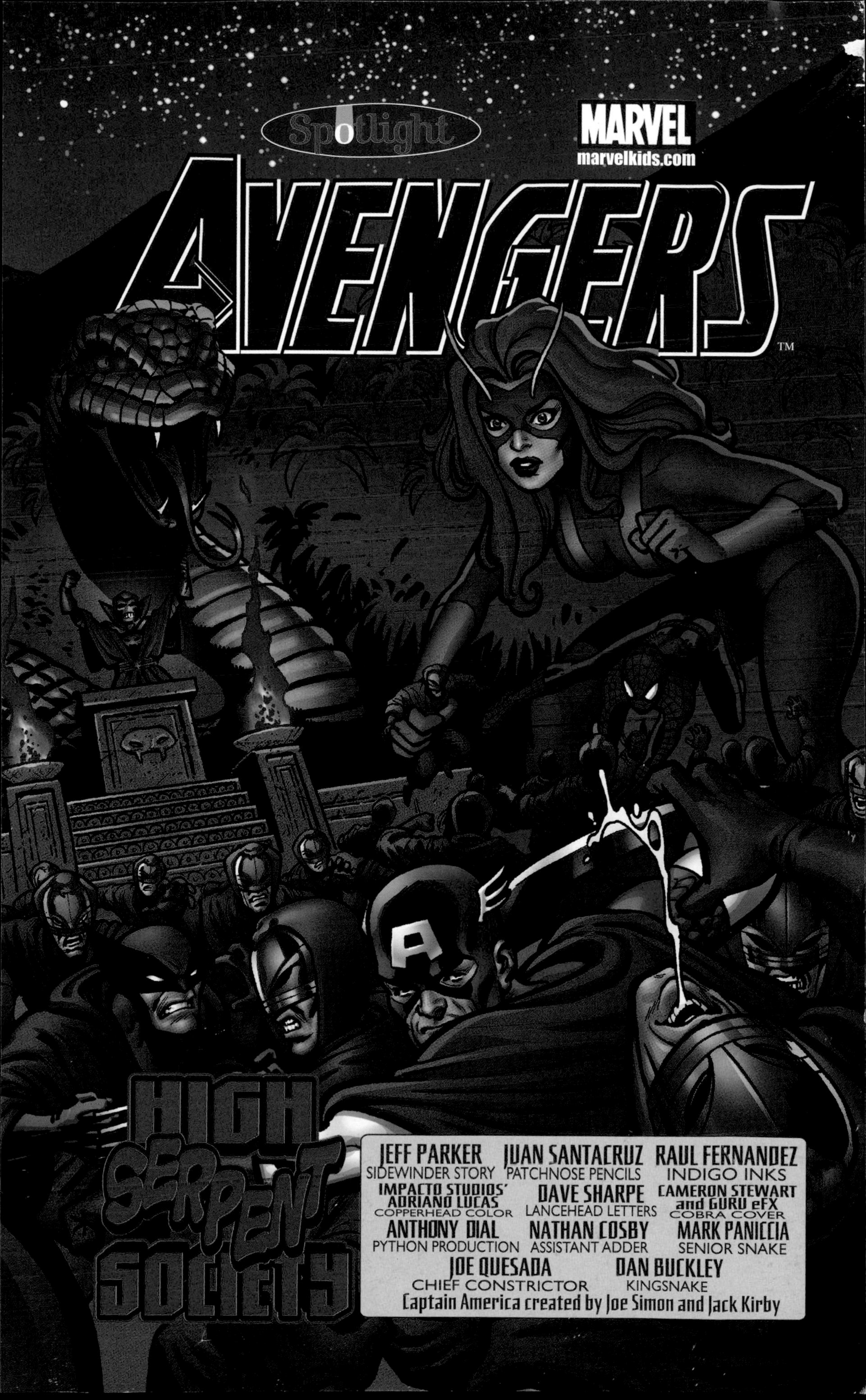
Spotlight
MARVEL
marvelkids.com
AVENGERS™
HIGH SERPENT SOCIETY
JEFF PARKER
SIDEWINDER STORY
JUAN SANTACRUZ
PATCHNOSE PENCILS
RAUL FERNANDEZ
INDIGO INKS
IMPACTO STUDIOS' ADRIANO LUCAS
COPPERHEAD COLOR
DAVE SHARPE
LANCEHEAD LETTERS
CAMERON STEWART and GURU eFX
COBRA COVER
ANTHONY DIAL
PYTHON PRODUCTION
NATHAN COSBY
ASSISTANT ADDER
MARK PANICCIA
SENIOR SNAKE
JOE QUESADA
CHIEF CONSTRICTOR
DAN BUCKLEY
KINGSNAKE
Captain America created by Joe Simon and Jack Kirby

visit us at www.abdopublishing.com

Reinforced library bound edition published in 2013 by Spotlight, a division of the ABDO Group, 8000 West 78th Street, Edina, Minnesota 55439. Spotlight produces high-quality reinforced library bound editions for schools and libraries. Published by agreement with Marvel Entertainment, LLC. The stories, characters, and incidents mentioned are entirely fictional. All rights reserved. Used under authorization.

Printed in the United States of America, North Mankato, Minnesota.
052012
092012
♻ This book contains at least 10% recycled materials.

marvelkids.com

TM & © 2012 Marvel & Subs.

Library of Congress Cataloging-in-Publication Data

Parker, Jeff, 1966-

High Serpent Society / story by Jeff Parker ; art by Juan Santacruz. -- Reinforced library bound ed.

    p. cm. -- (Avengers)

"Marvel."

Summary: The Avengers are recruited by the evil Serpent Society, which uses snake venom to control its inductees.

ISBN 978-1-61479-015-0 (alk. paper)

1. Graphic novels. [1. Graphic novels. 2. Superheroes--Fiction. 3. Secret societies--Fiction.] I. Santacruz, Juan, ill. II. Title.

PZ7.7.P252Hig 2012

741.5'973--dc23

2012000927

ISBN 978-1-61479-015-0 (reinforced library edition)

All Spotlight books are reinforced library binding and manufactured in the United States of America.

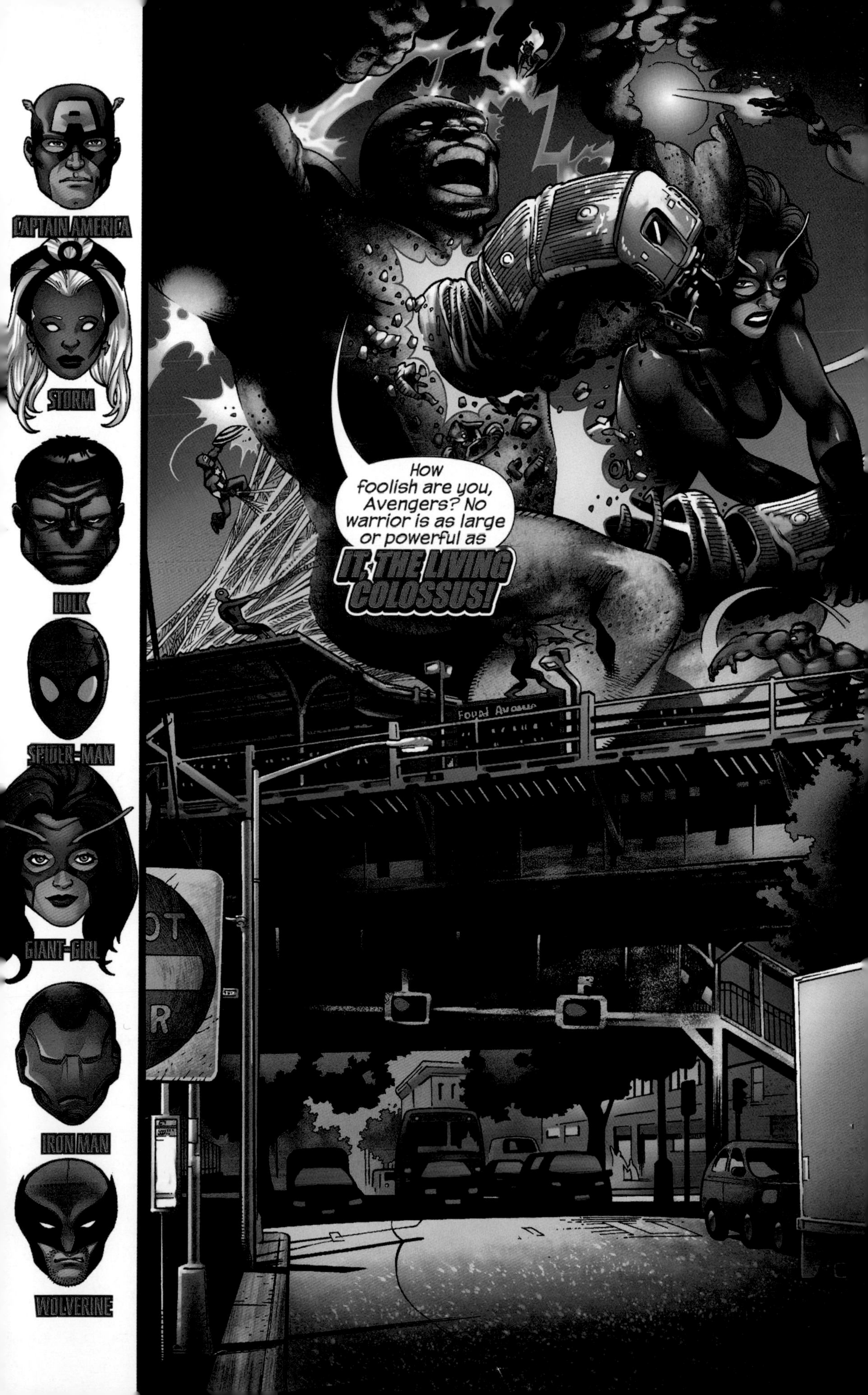
CAPTAIN AMERICA
STORM
HULK
SPIDER-MAN
GIANT-GIRL
IRON MAN
WOLVERINE
How foolish are you, Avengers? No warrior is as large or powerful as IT, THE LIVING COLOSSUS!

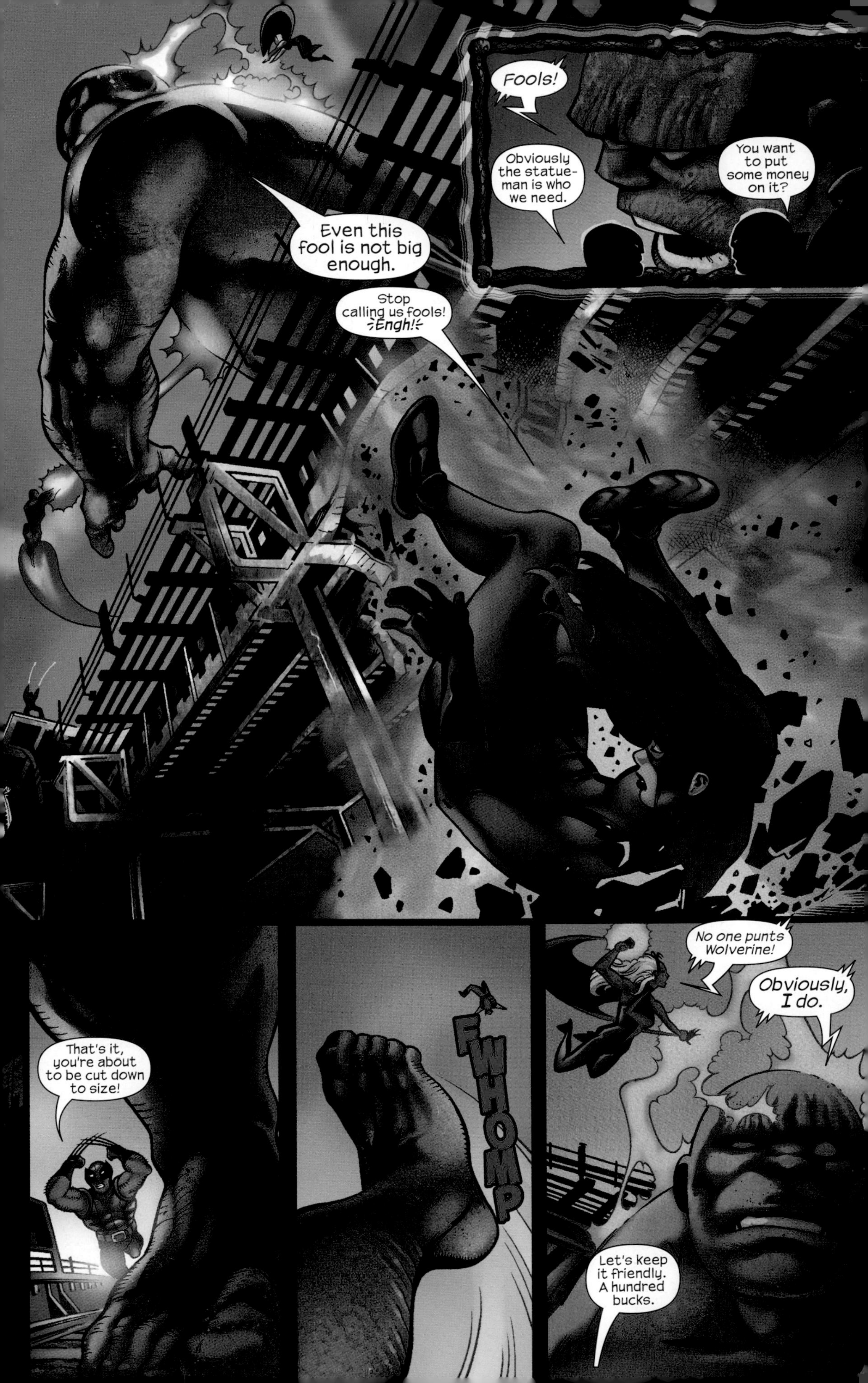
Fools!
Obviously the statue-man is who we need.
You want to put some money on it?
Even this fool is not big enough.
Stop calling us fools! Engh!
That's it, you're about to be cut down to size!
FWHOMP
No one punts Wolverine!
Obviously, I do.
Let's keep it friendly. A hundred bucks.

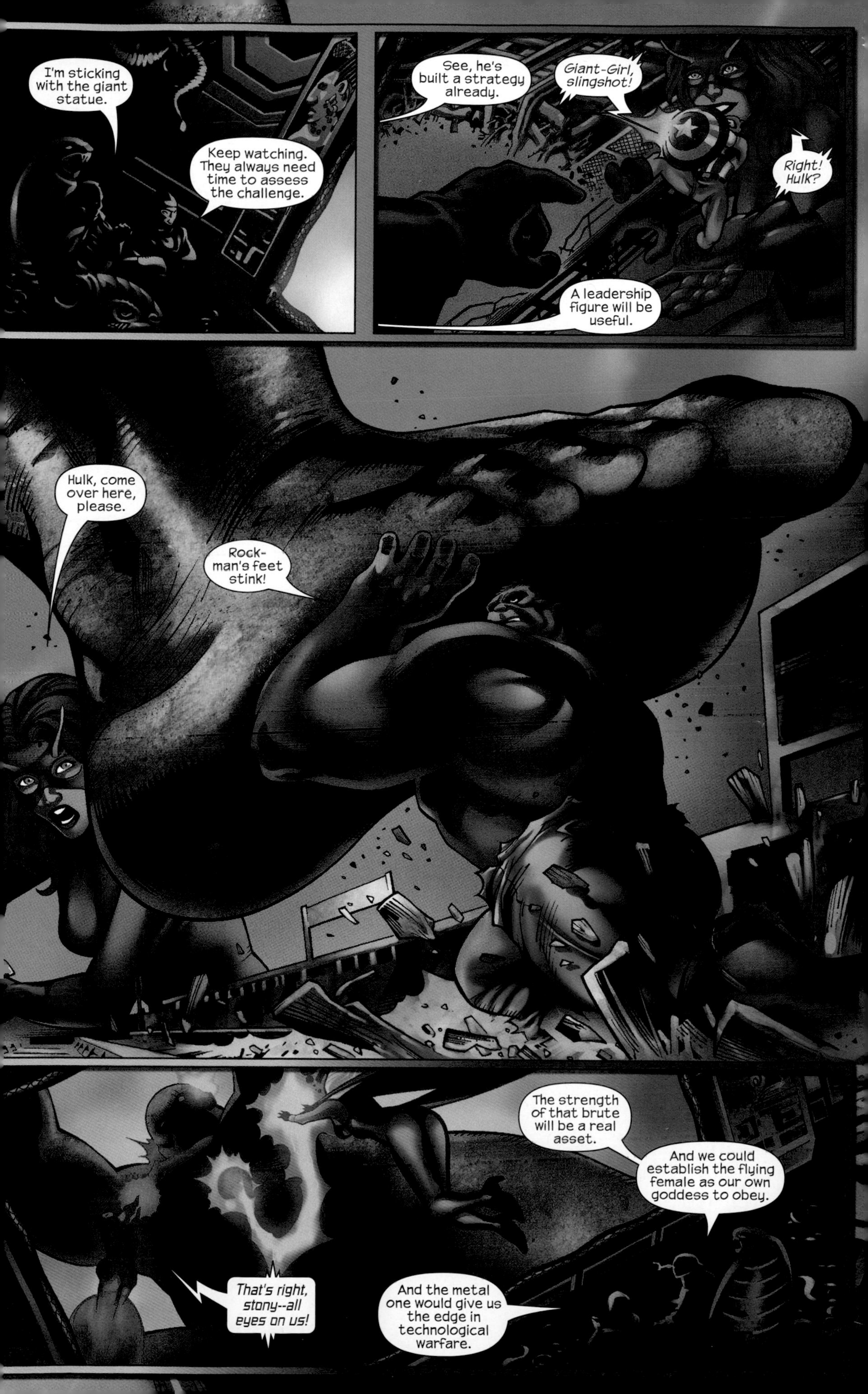
I'm sticking with the giant statue.
Keep watching. They always need time to assess the challenge.
See, he's built a strategy already.
Giant-Girl, slingshot!
Right! Hulk?
A leadership figure will be useful.
Hulk, come over here, please.
Rock-man's feet stink!
The strength of that brute will be a real asset.
And we could establish the flying female as our own goddess to obey.
That's right, stony--all eyes on us!
And the metal one would give us the edge in technological warfare.

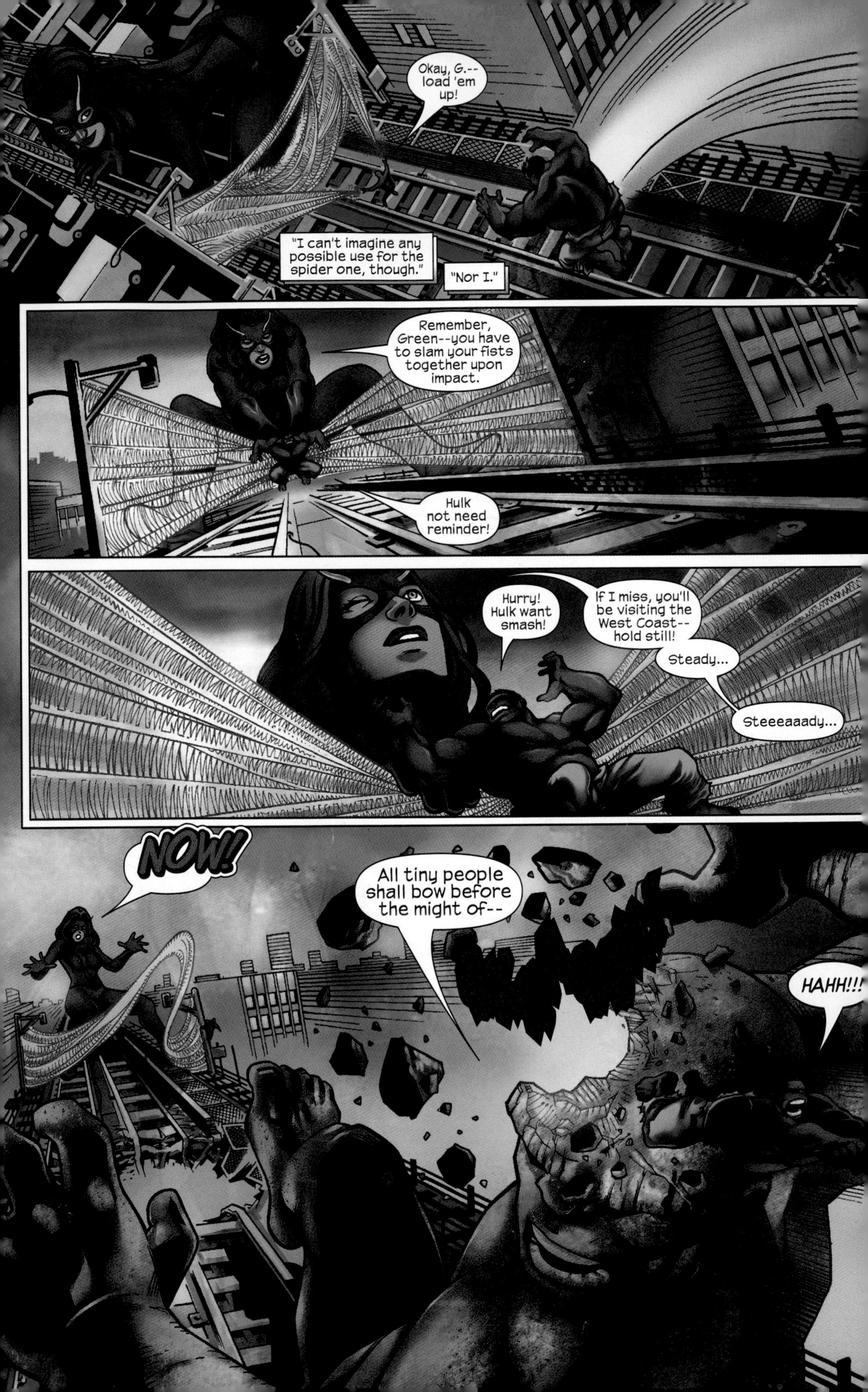
Okay, G.-- load 'em up!
"I can't imagine any possible use for the spider one, though."
"Nor I."
Remember, Green--you have to slam your fists together upon impact.
Hulk not need reminder!
Hurry! Hulk want smash!
If I miss, you'll be visiting the West Coast-- hold still!
Steady...
Steeeaaady...
NOW!
All tiny people shall bow before the might of--
HAHH!!!

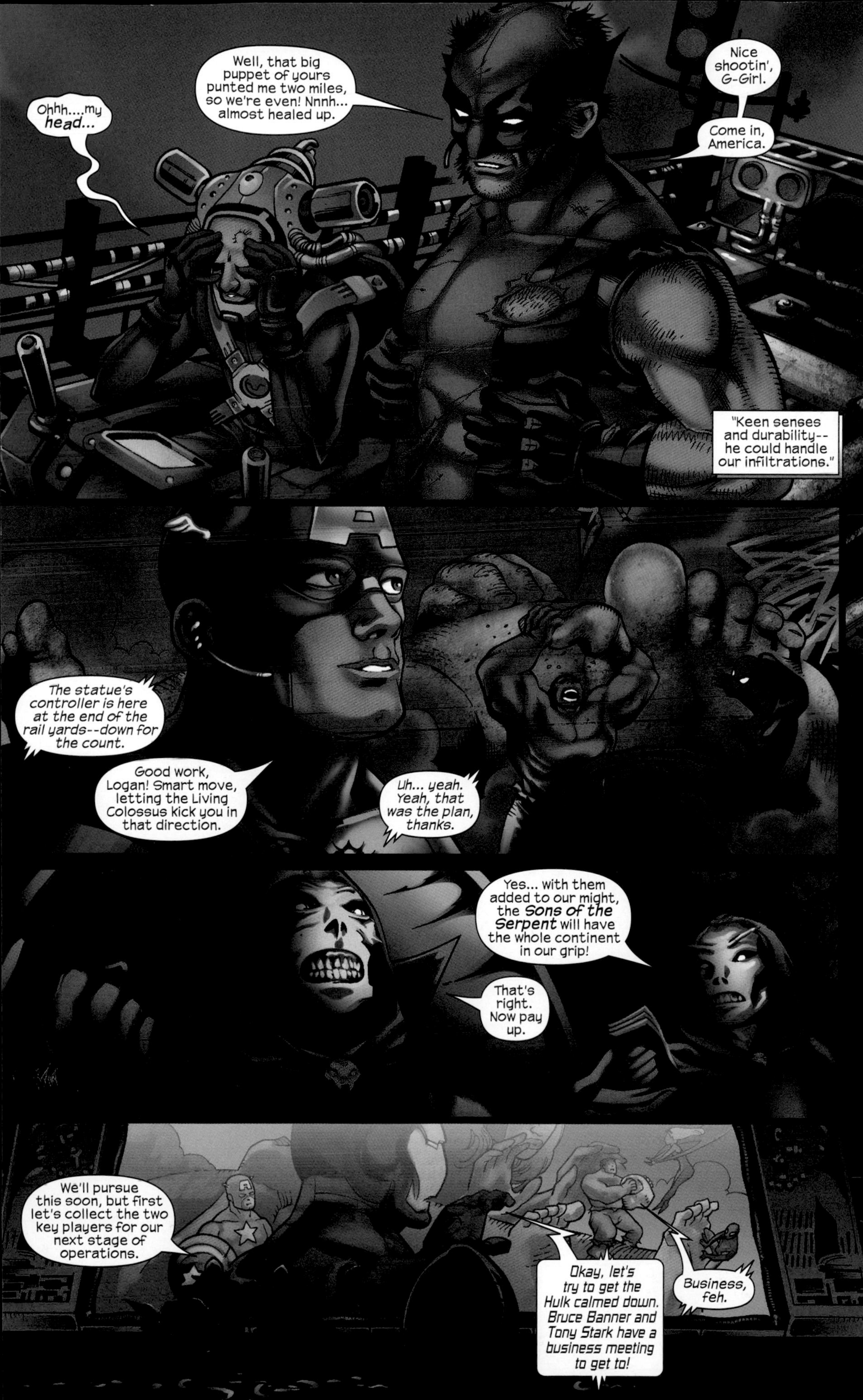
Ohhh....my head...
Well, that big puppet of yours punted me two miles, so we're even! Nnnh... almost healed up.
Nice shootin', G-Girl.
Come in, America.
"Keen senses and durability--he could handle our infiltrations."
The statue's controller is here at the end of the rail yards--down for the count.
Good work, Logan! Smart move, letting the Living Colossus kick you in that direction.
Uh... yeah. Yeah, that was the plan, thanks.
Yes... with them added to our might, the Sons of the Serpent will have the whole continent in our grip!
That's right. Now pay up.
We'll pursue this soon, but first let's collect the two key players for our next stage of operations.
Okay, let's try to get the Hulk calmed down. Bruce Banner and Tony Stark have a business meeting to get to!
Business, feh.

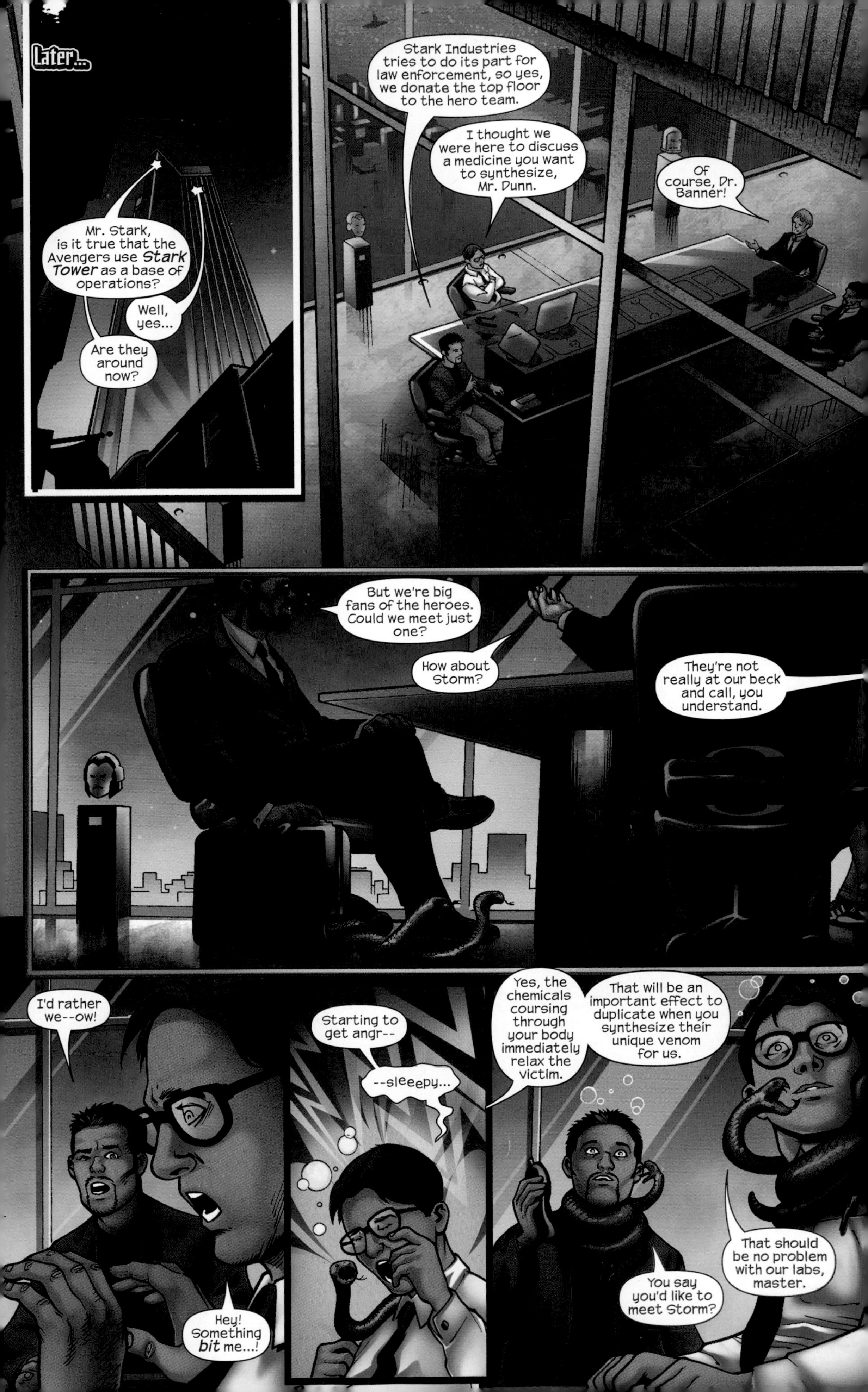
Later...
Mr. Stark, is it true that the Avengers use Stark Tower as a base of operations?
Well, yes...
Are they around now?
Stark Industries tries to do its part for law enforcement, so yes, we donate the top floor to the hero team.
I thought we were here to discuss a medicine you want to synthesize, Mr. Dunn.
Of course, Dr. Banner!
But we're big fans of the heroes. Could we meet just one?
How about Storm?
They're not really at our beck and call, you understand.
I'd rather we--ow!
Hey! Something bit me...!
Starting to get angr--
--sleeepy...
Yes, the chemicals coursing through your body immediately relax the victim.
That will be an important effect to duplicate when you synthesize their unique venom for us.
You say you'd like to meet Storm?
That should be no problem with our labs, master.

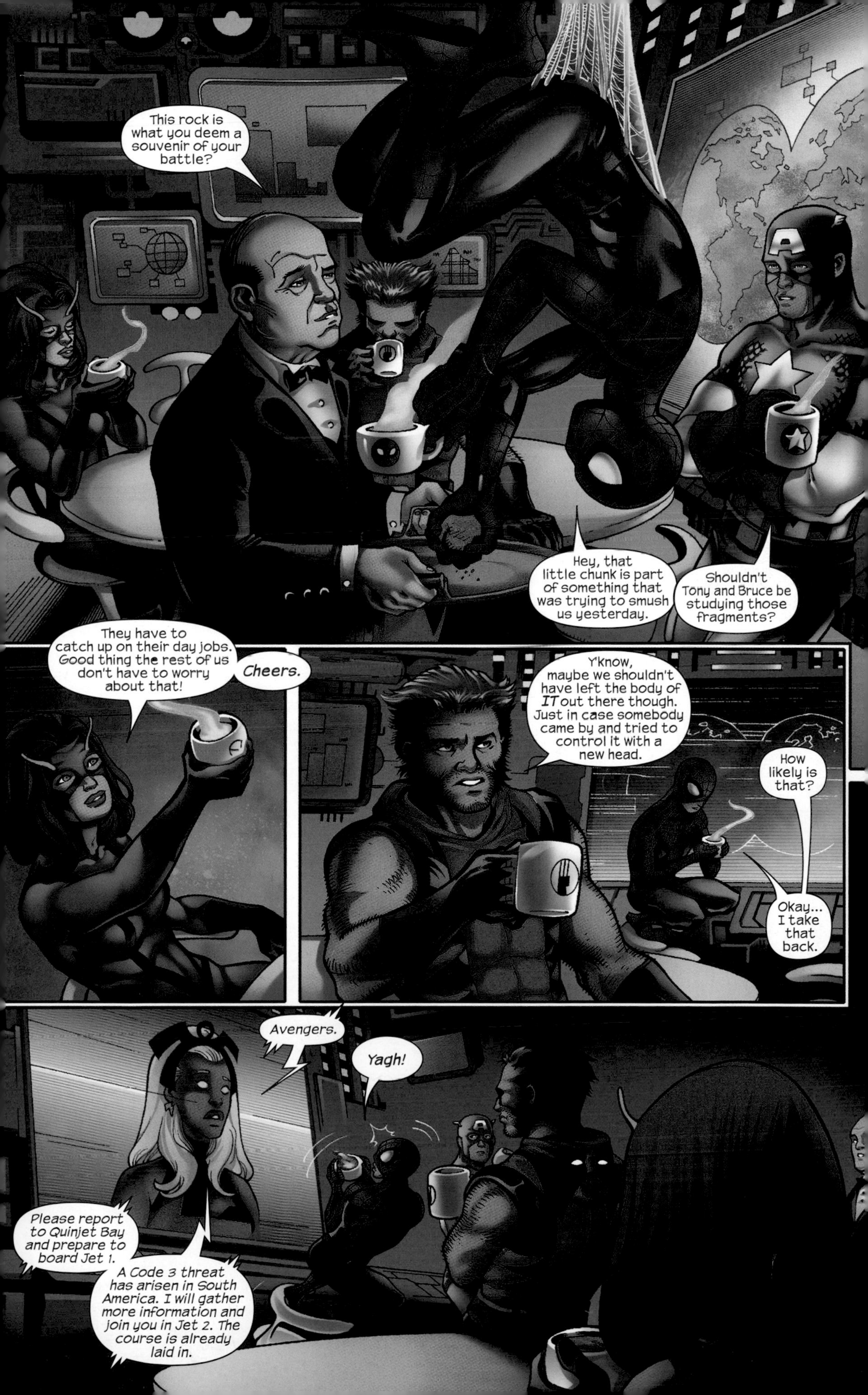
This rock is what you deem a souvenir of your battle?
Hey, that little chunk is part of something that was trying to smush us yesterday.
Shouldn't Tony and Bruce be studying those fragments?
They have to catch up on their day jobs. Good thing the rest of us don't have to worry about that!
Cheers.
Y'know, maybe we shouldn't have left the body of IT out there though. Just in case somebody came by and tried to control it with a new head.
How likely is that?
Okay... I take that back.
Avengers.
Yagh!
Please report to Quinjet Bay and prepare to board Jet 1.
A Code 3 threat has arisen in South America. I will gather more information and join you in Jet 2. The course is already laid in.

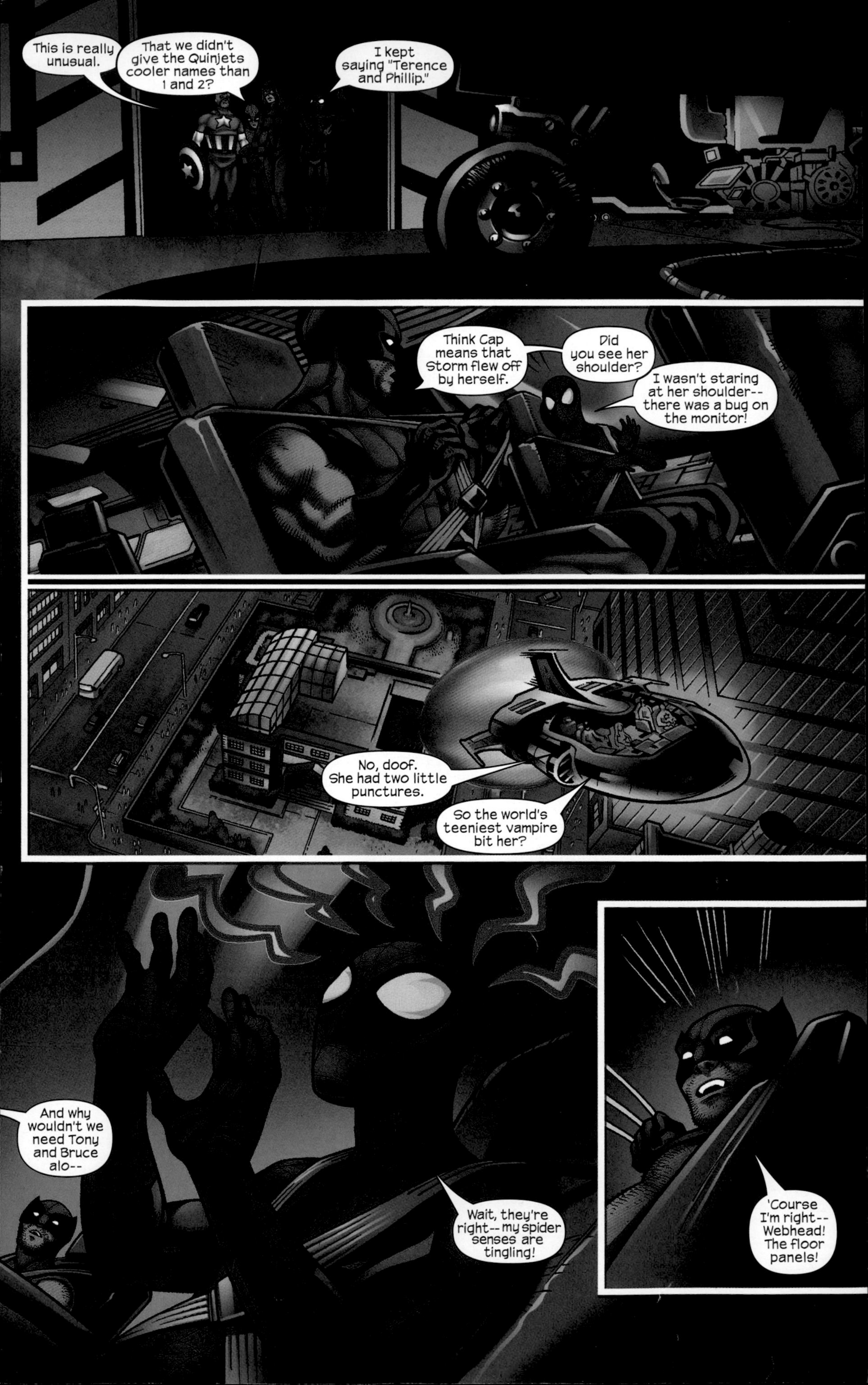

This is really unusual.
That we didn't give the Quinjets cooler names than 1 and 2?
I kept saying "Terence and Phillip."
Think Cap means that Storm flew off by herself.
Did you see her shoulder?
I wasn't staring at her shoulder-- there was a bug on the monitor!
No, doof. She had two little punctures.
So the world's teeniest vampire bit her?
And why wouldn't we need Tony and Bruce alo--
Wait, they're right-- my spider senses are tingling!
'Course I'm right-- Webhead! The floor panels!

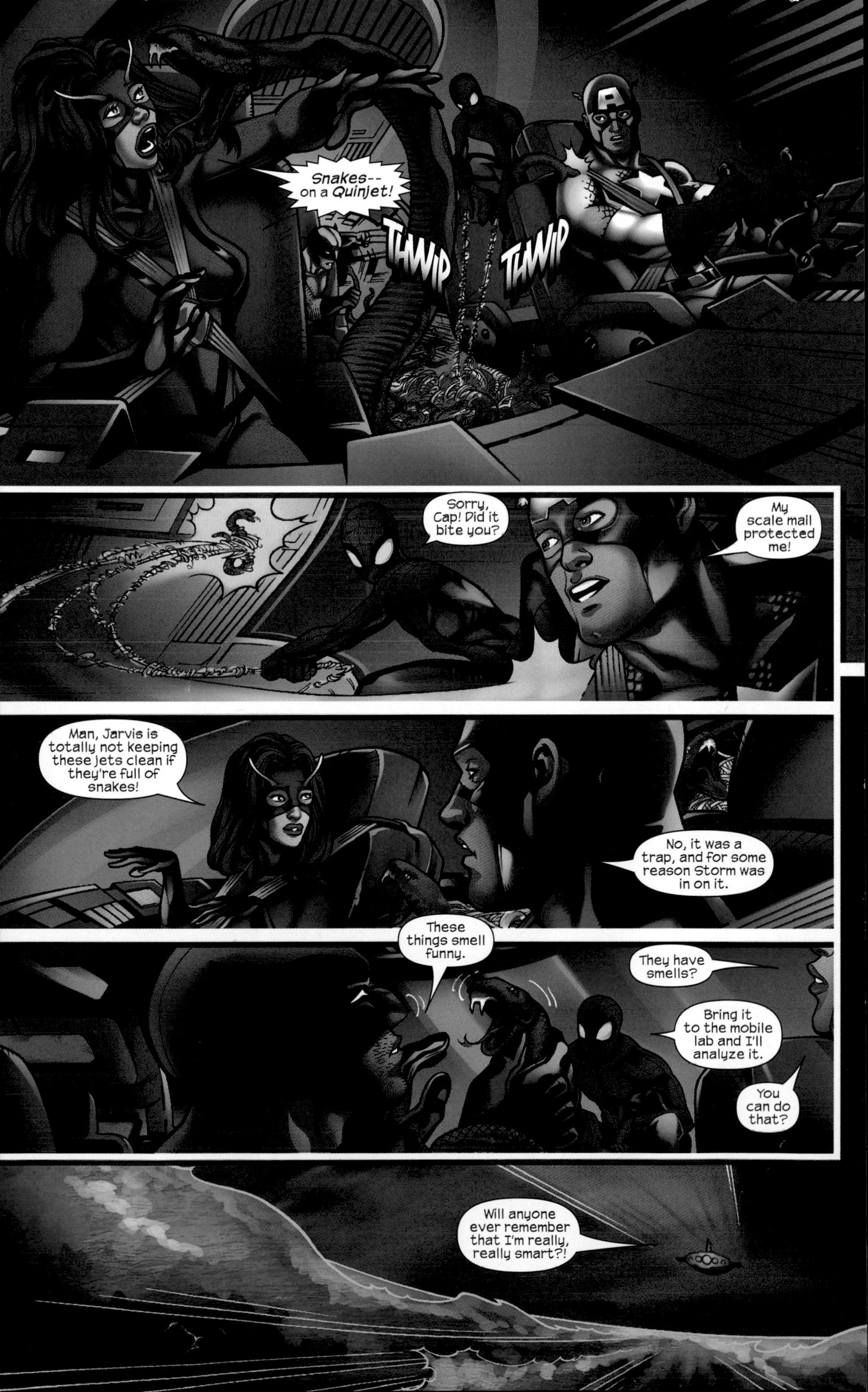
Snakes-- on a Quinjet!
THWIP
THWIP
Sorry, Cap! Did it bite you?
My scale mail protected me!
Man, Jarvis is totally not keeping these jets clean if they're full of snakes!
No, it was a trap, and for some reason Storm was in on it.
These things smell funny.
They have smells?
Bring it to the mobile lab and I'll analyze it.
You can do that?
Will anyone ever remember that I'm really, really smart?!

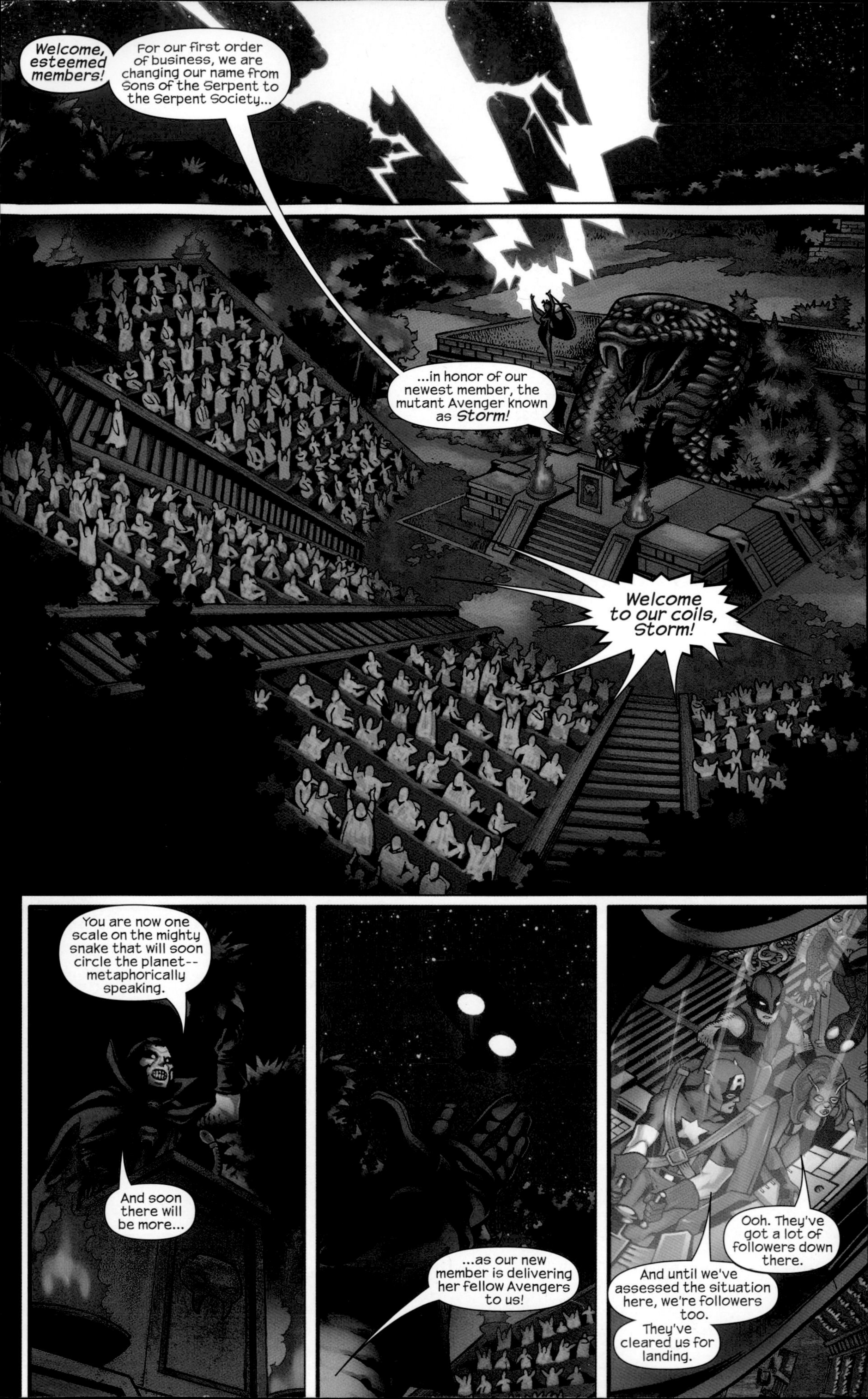
Welcome, esteemed members!
For our first order of business, we are changing our name from Sons of the Serpent to the Serpent Society...
...in honor of our newest member, the mutant Avenger known as Storm!
Welcome to our coils, Storm!
You are now one scale on the mighty snake that will soon circle the planet-- metaphorically speaking.
And soon there will be more...
...as our new member is delivering her fellow Avengers to us!
Ooh. They've got a lot of followers down there.
And until we've assessed the situation here, we're followers too.
They've cleared us for landing.

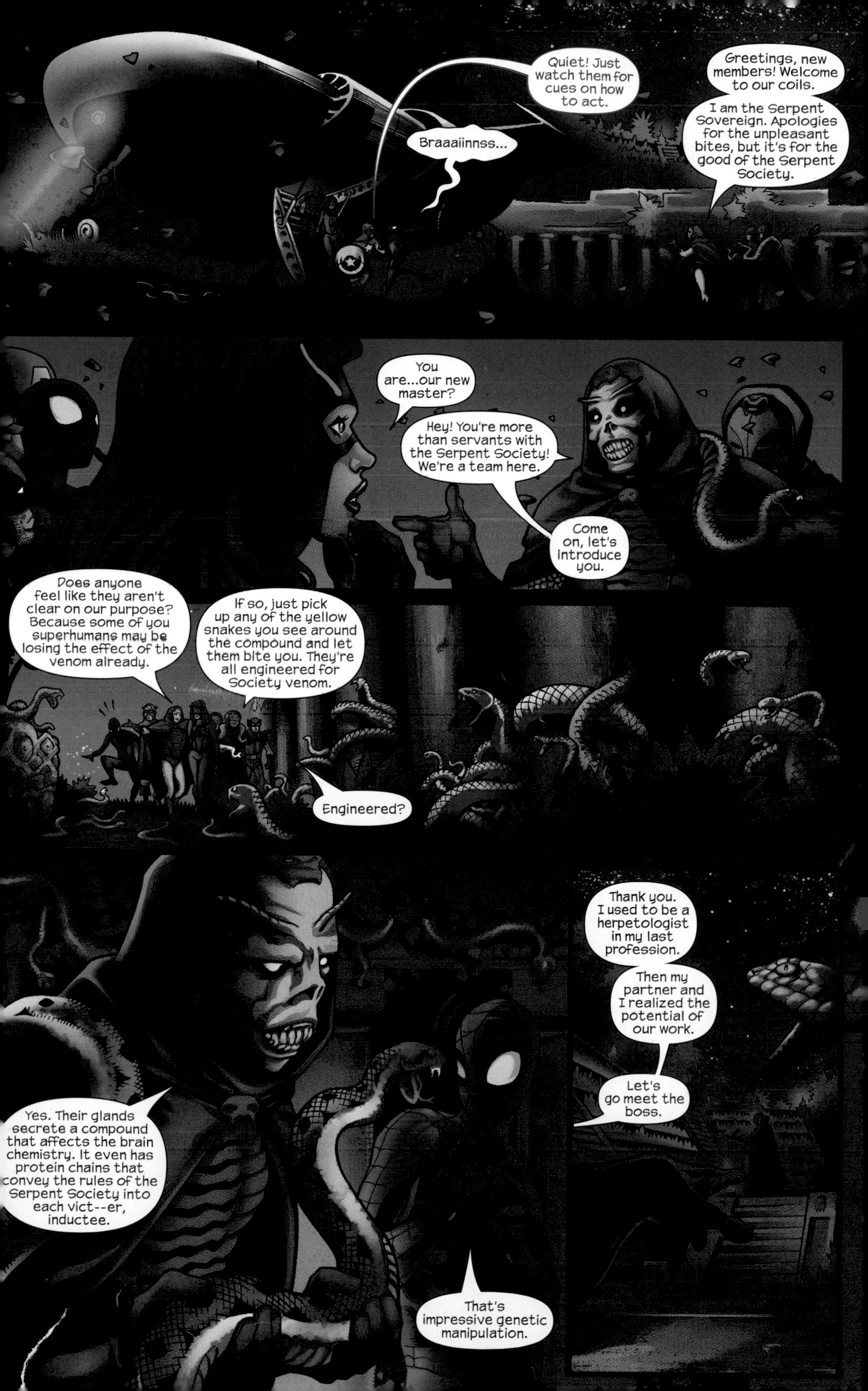
Quiet! Just watch them for cues on how to act.
Braaaiinnss...
Greetings, new members! Welcome to our coils.
I am the Serpent Sovereign. Apologies for the unpleasant bites, but it's for the good of the Serpent Society.
You are...our new master?
Hey! You're more than servants with the Serpent Society! We're a team here.
Come on, let's introduce you.
Does anyone feel like they aren't clear on our purpose? Because some of you superhumans may be losing the effect of the venom already.
If so, just pick up any of the yellow snakes you see around the compound and let them bite you. They're all engineered for Society venom.
Engineered?
Yes. Their glands secrete a compound that affects the brain chemistry. It even has protein chains that convey the rules of the Serpent Society into each vict--er, inductee.
That's impressive genetic manipulation.
Thank you. I used to be a herpetologist in my last profession.
Then my partner and I realized the potential of our work.
Let's go meet the boss.

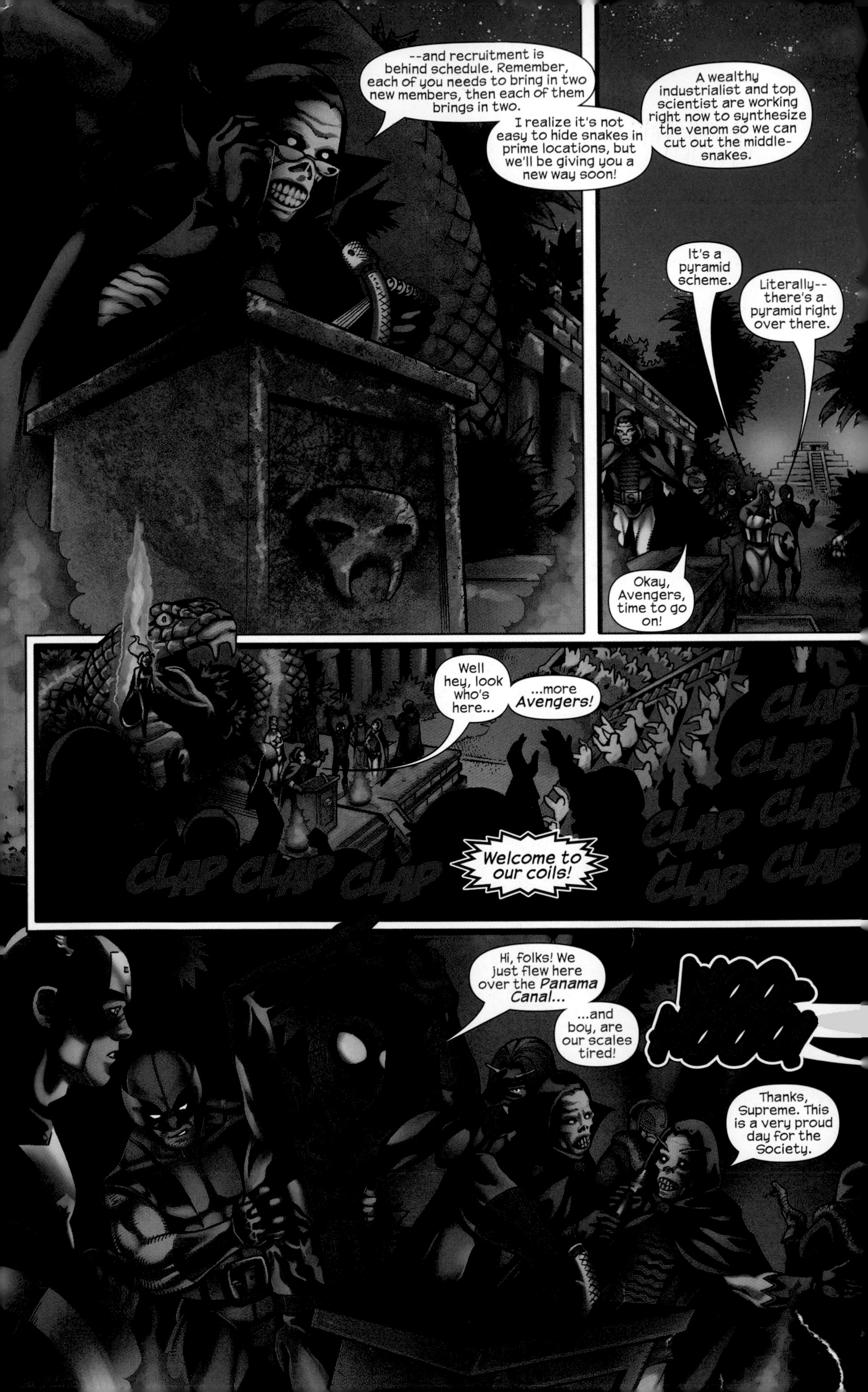
--and recruitment is behind schedule. Remember, each of you needs to bring in two new members, then each of them brings in two.
I realize it's not easy to hide snakes in prime locations, but we'll be giving you a new way soon!
A wealthy industrialist and top scientist are working right now to synthesize the venom so we can cut out the middle-snakes.
It's a pyramid scheme.
Literally-- there's a pyramid right over there.
Okay, Avengers, time to go on!
Well hey, look who's here...
...more Avengers!
CLAP CLAP CLAP
Welcome to our coils!
CLAP CLAP CLAP CLAP CLAP CLAP CLAP
Hi, folks! We just flew here over the Panama Canal...
...and boy, are our scales tired!
Thanks, Supreme. This is a very proud day for the Society.

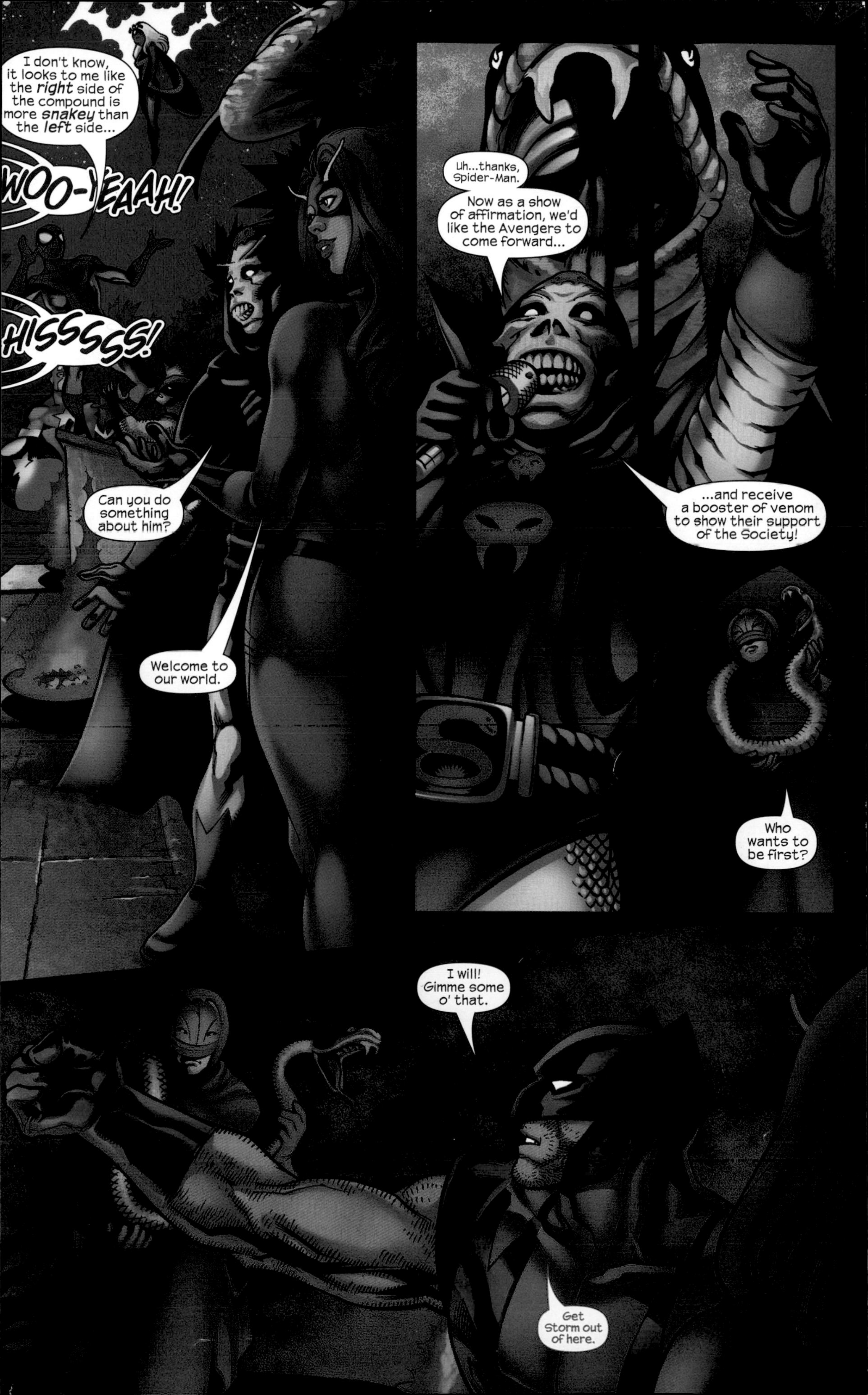
I don't know, it looks to me like the *right* side of the compound is more *snakey* than the *left* side...
WOO-YEAAH!
HISSSSSS!
Can you do something about him?
Welcome to our world.
Uh...thanks, Spider-Man.
Now as a show of affirmation, we'd like the Avengers to come forward...
...and receive a booster of venom to show their support of the Society!
Who wants to be first?
I will! Gimme some o' that.
Get Storm out of here.

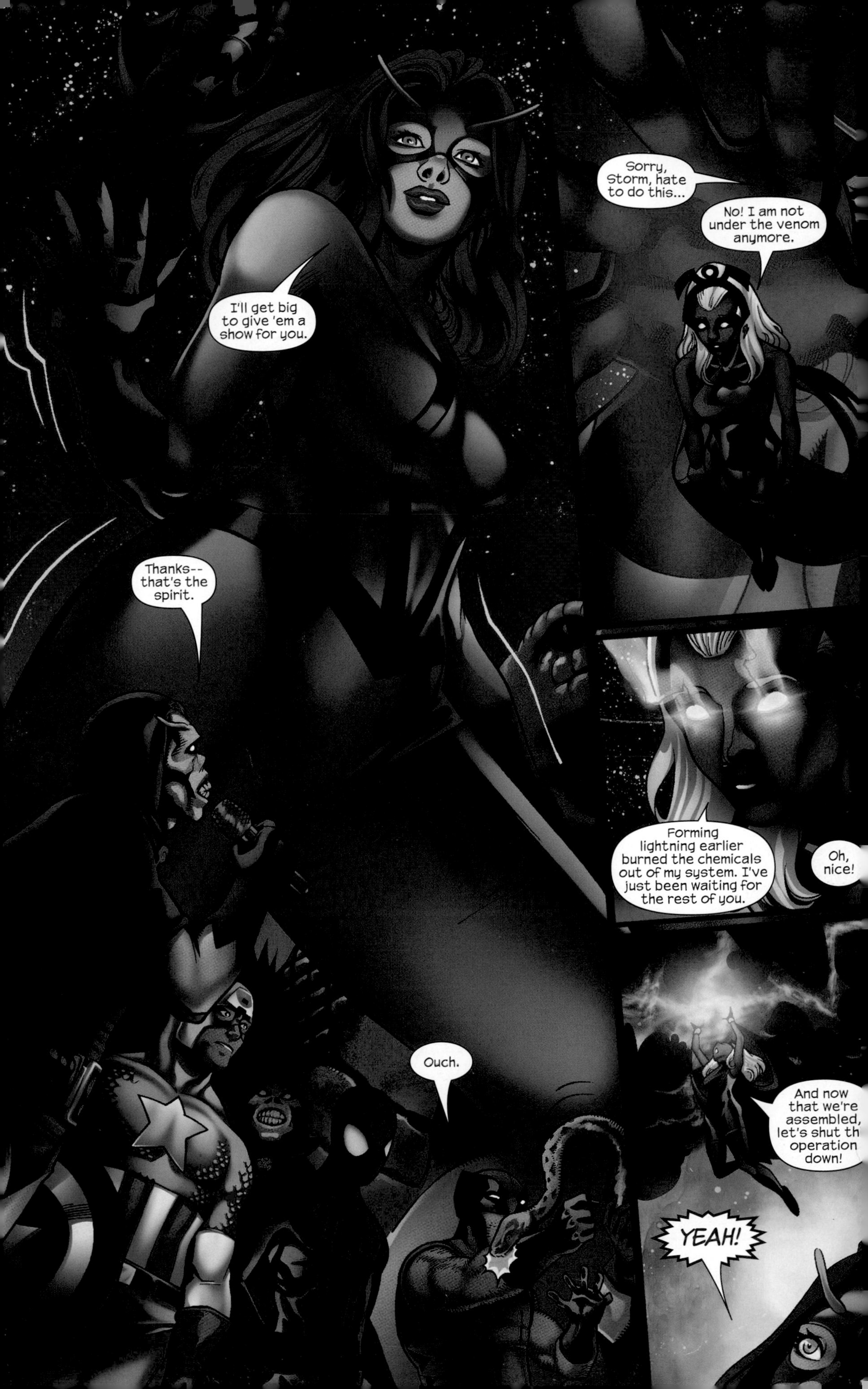
I'll get big to give 'em a show for you.
Thanks-- that's the spirit.
Ouch.
Sorry, Storm, hate to do this...
No! I am not under the venom anymore.
Forming lightning earlier burned the chemicals out of my system. I've just been waiting for the rest of you.
Oh, nice!
And now that we're assembled, let's shut th operation down!
YEAH!

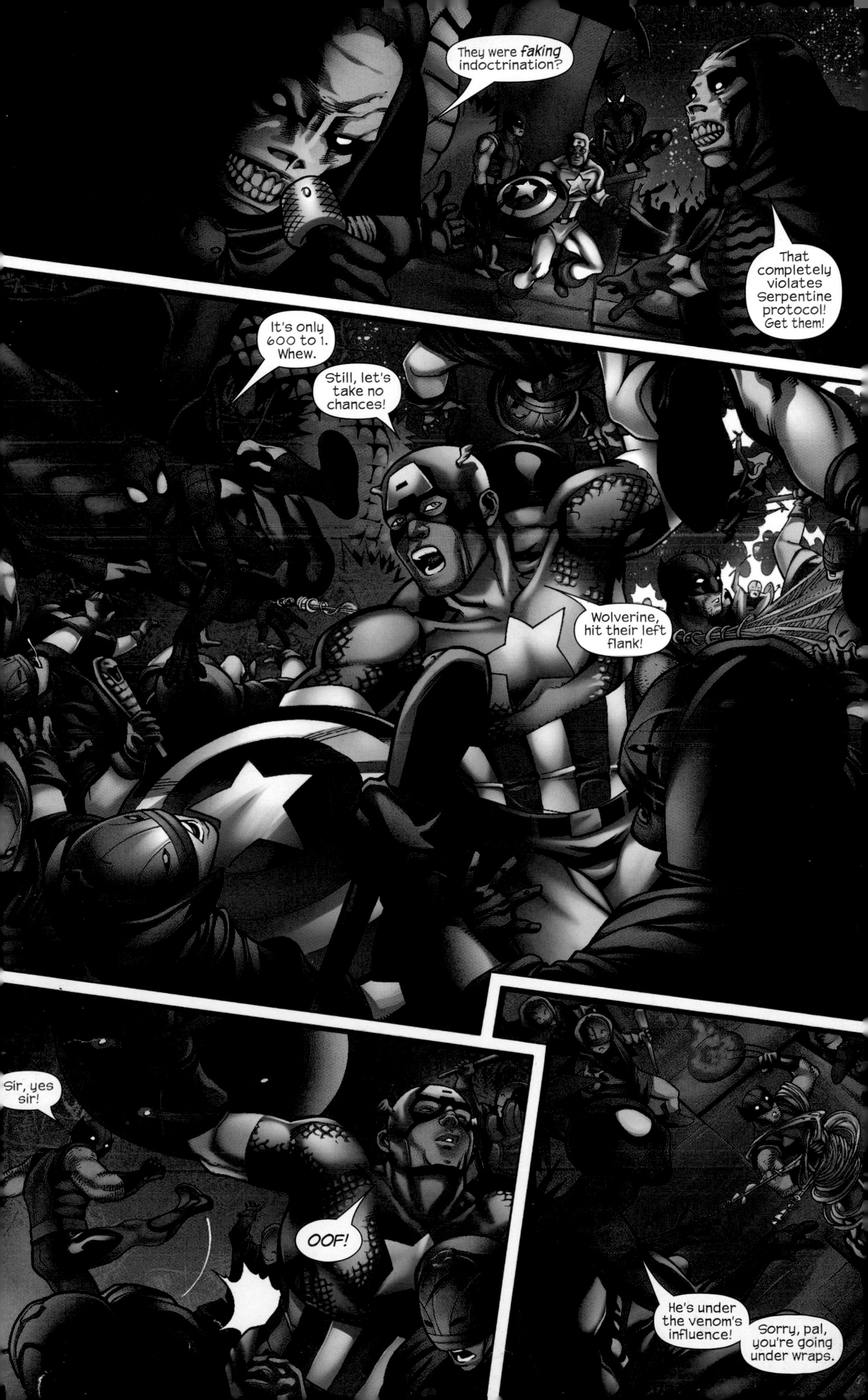
They were *faking* indoctrination?
That completely violates Serpentine protocol! Get them!
It's only 600 to 1. Whew.
Still, let's take no chances!
Wolverine, hit their left flank!
Sir, yes sir!
OOF!
He's under the venom's influence!
Sorry, pal, you're going under wraps.

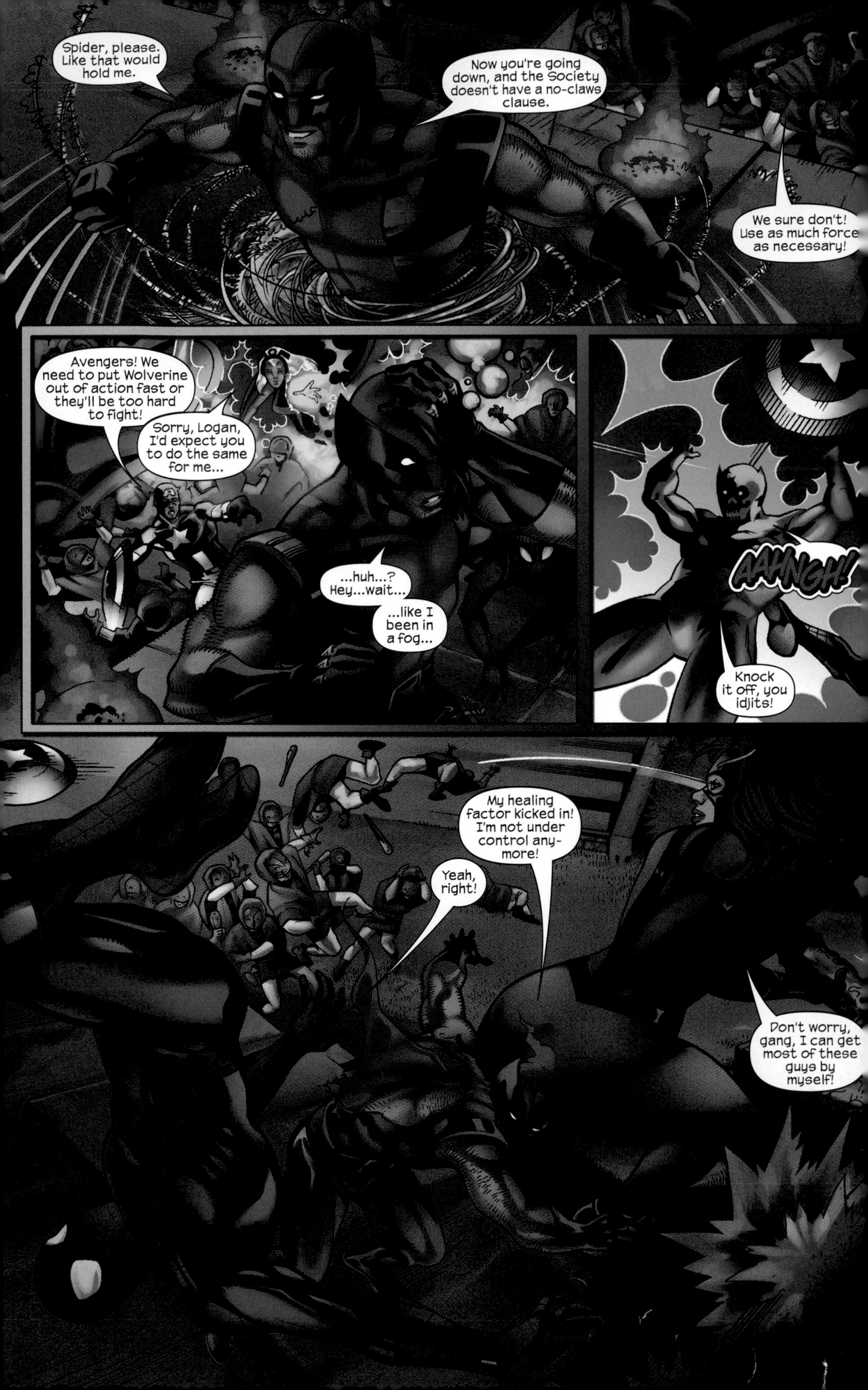
Spider, please. Like that would hold me.
Now you're going down, and the Society doesn't have a no-claws clause.
We sure don't! Use as much force as necessary!
Avengers! We need to put Wolverine out of action fast or they'll be too hard to fight!
Sorry, Logan, I'd expect you to do the same for me...
...huh...? Hey...wait...
...like I been in a fog...
AAHNGH!
Knock it off, you idjits!
My healing factor kicked in! I'm not under control any-more!
Yeah, right!
Don't worry, gang, I can get most of these guys by myself!

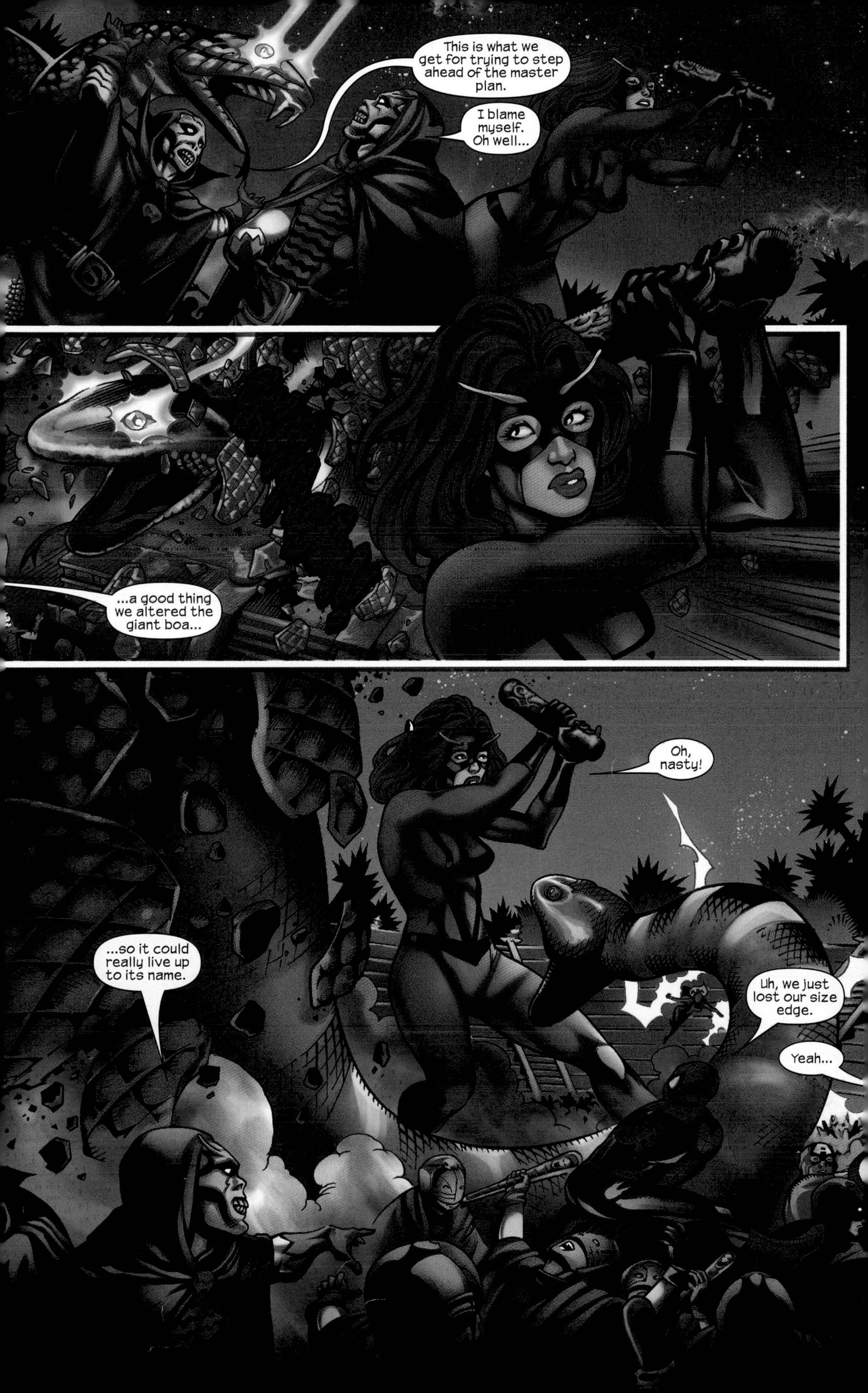
This is what we get for trying to step ahead of the master plan.
I blame myself. Oh well...
...a good thing we altered the giant boa...
Oh, nasty!
...so it could really live up to its name.
Uh, we just lost our size edge.
Yeah...

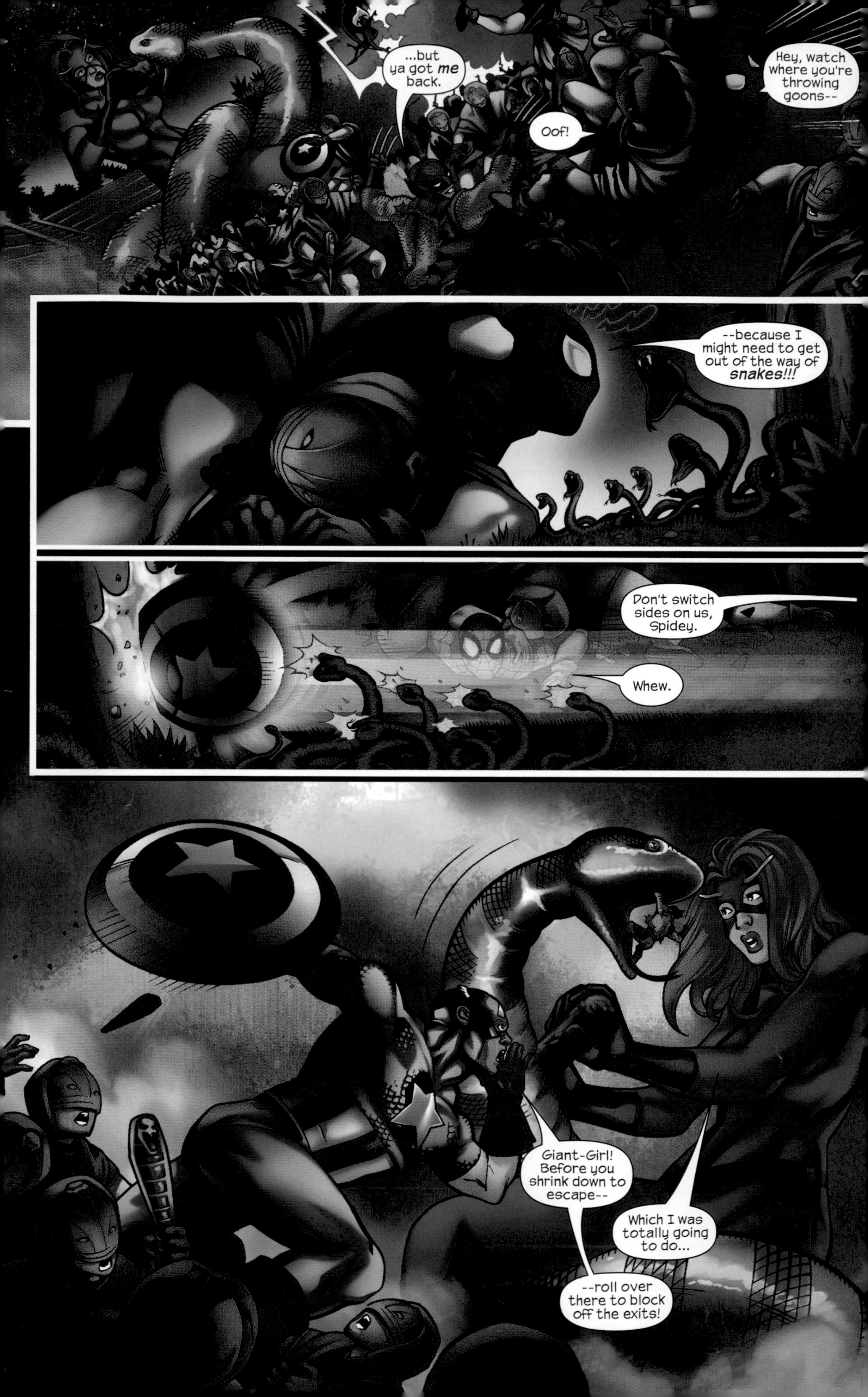
...but ya got *me* back.
Oof!
Hey, watch where you're throwing goons--
--because I might need to get out of the way of *snakes!!!*
Don't switch sides on us, Spidey.
Whew.
Giant-Girl! Before you shrink down to escape--
Which I was totally going to do...
--roll over there to block off the exits!

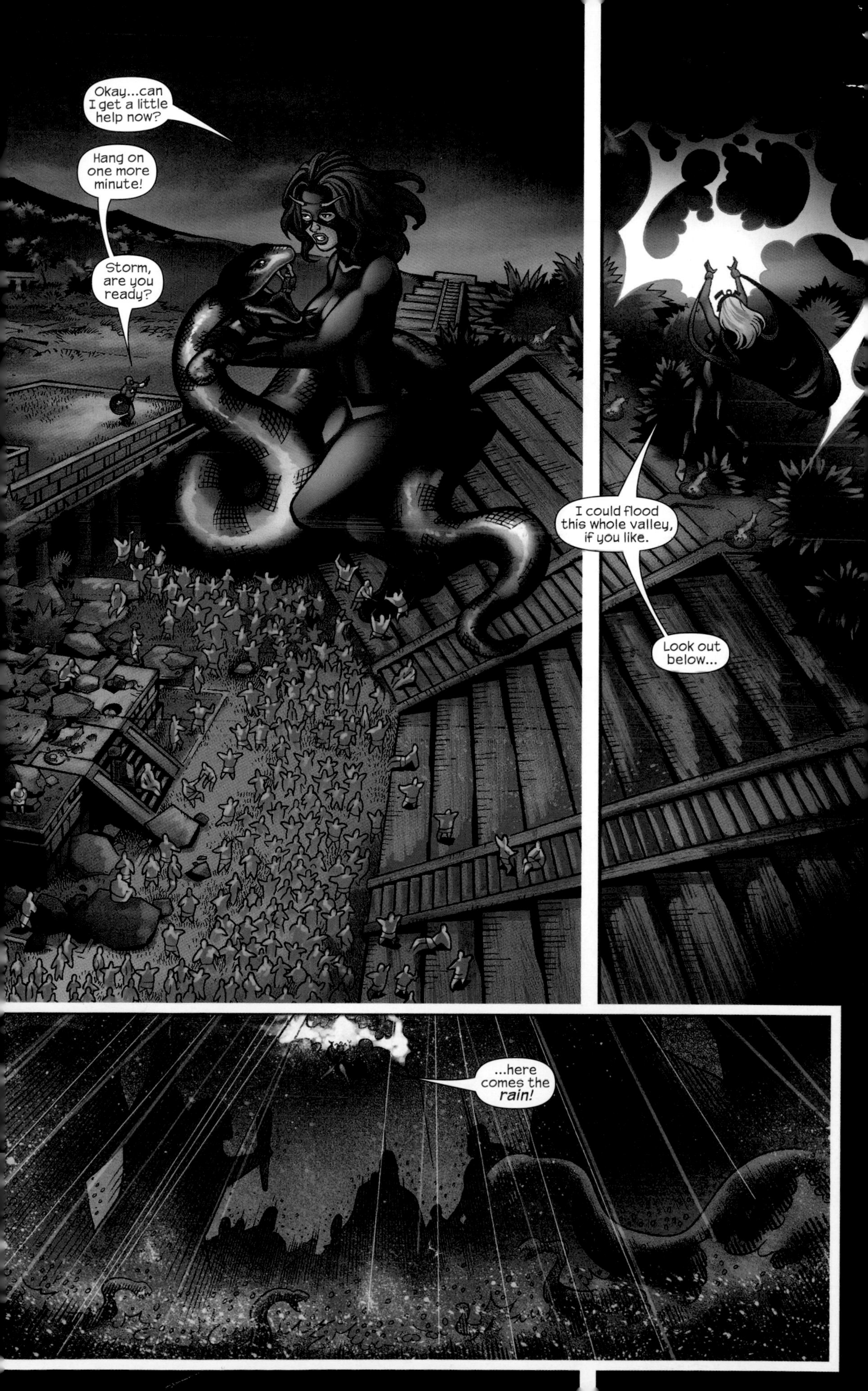
Okay...can I get a little help now?
Hang on one more minute!
Storm, are you ready?
I could flood this whole valley, if you like.
Look out below...
...here comes the *rain!*

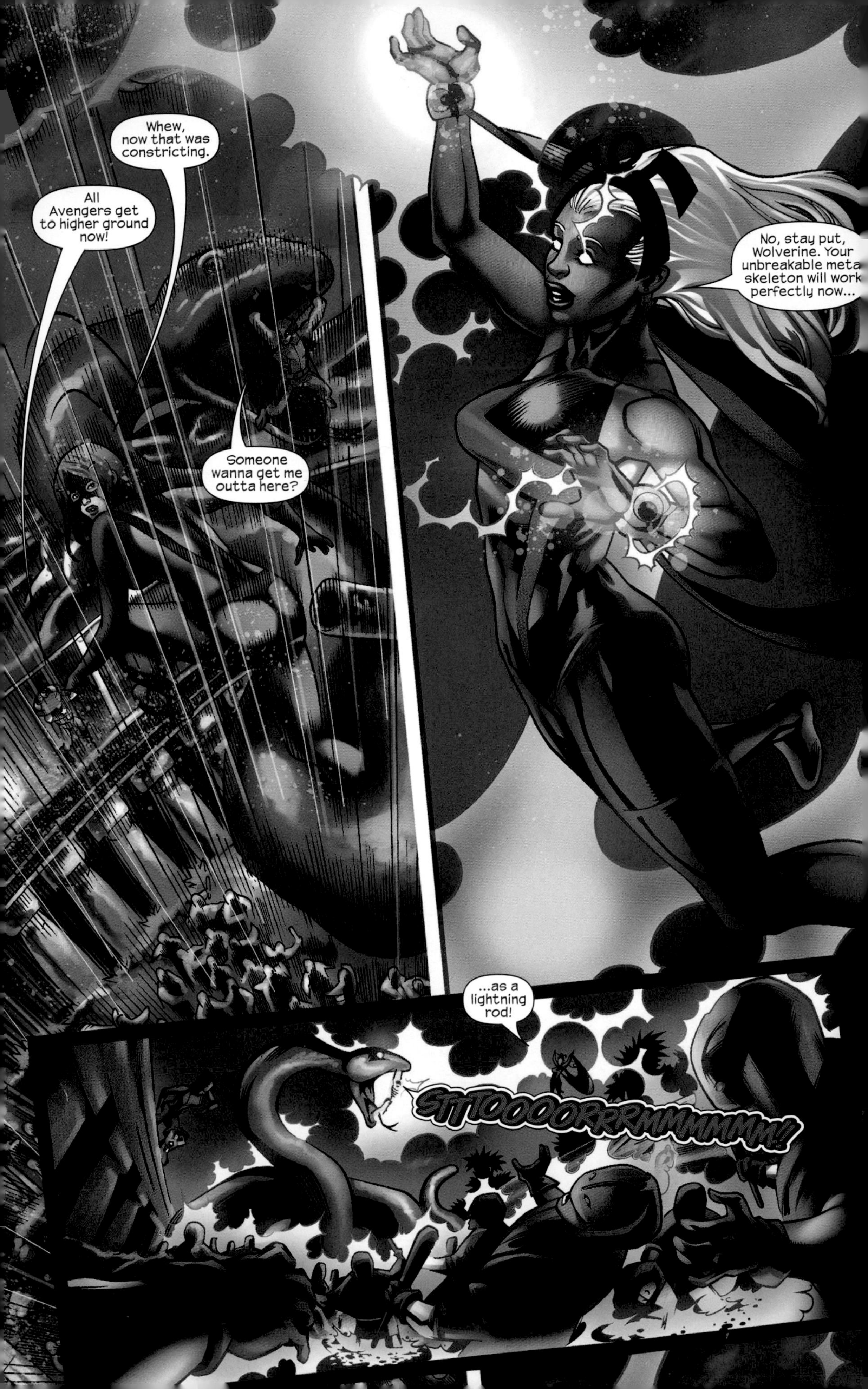
Whew, now that was constricting.
All Avengers get to higher ground now!
Someone wanna get me outta here?
No, stay put, Wolverine. Your unbreakable meta skeleton will work perfectly now...
...as a lightning rod!
STTTOOOOORRRMMMMMM!!

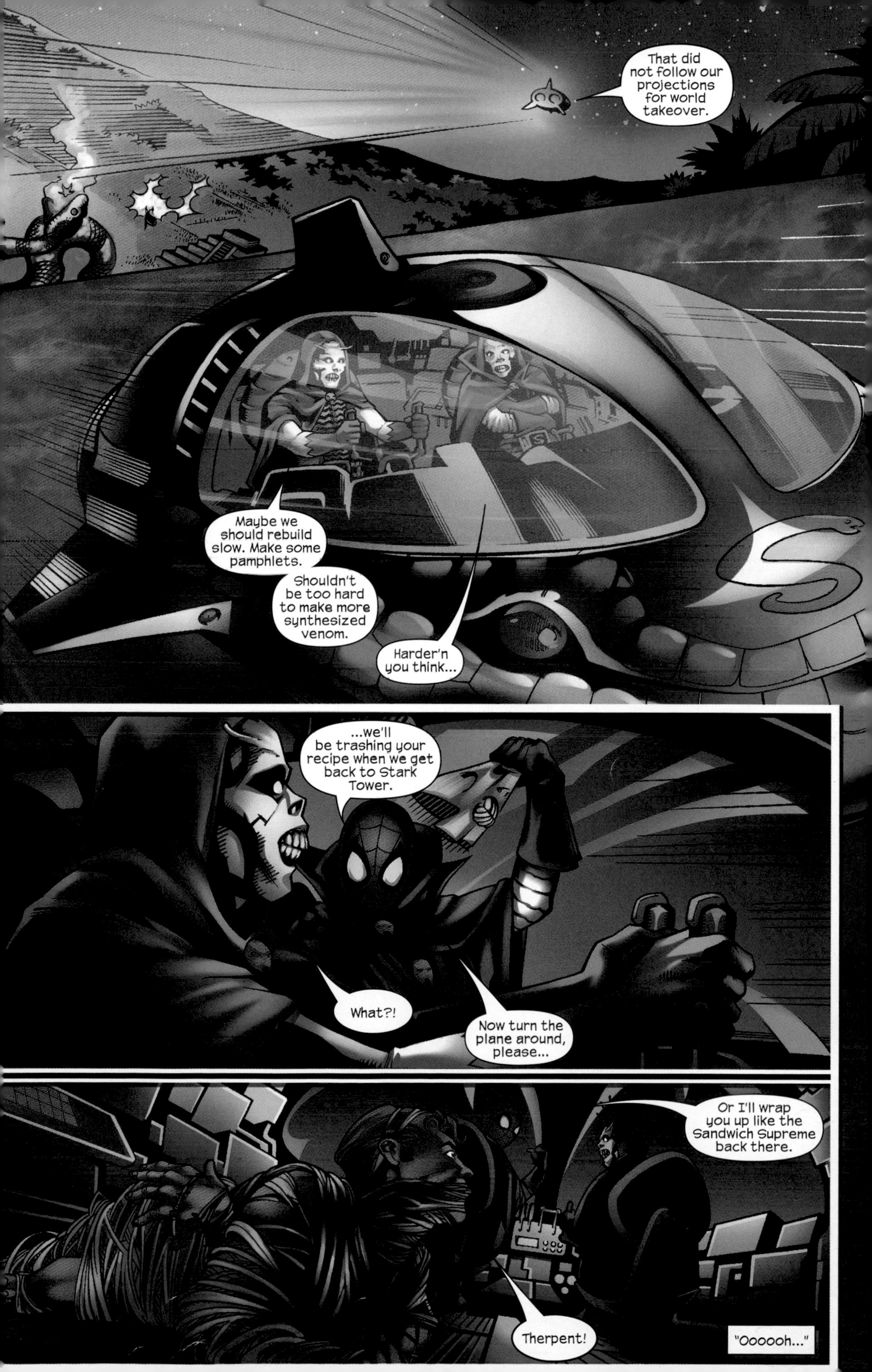
That did not follow our projections for world takeover.
Maybe we should rebuild slow. Make some pamphlets.
Shouldn't be too hard to make more synthesized venom.
Harder'n you think...
...we'll be trashing your recipe when we get back to Stark Tower.
What?!
Now turn the plane around, please...
Or I'll wrap you up like the Sandwich Supreme back there.
Therpent!
"Oooooh..."

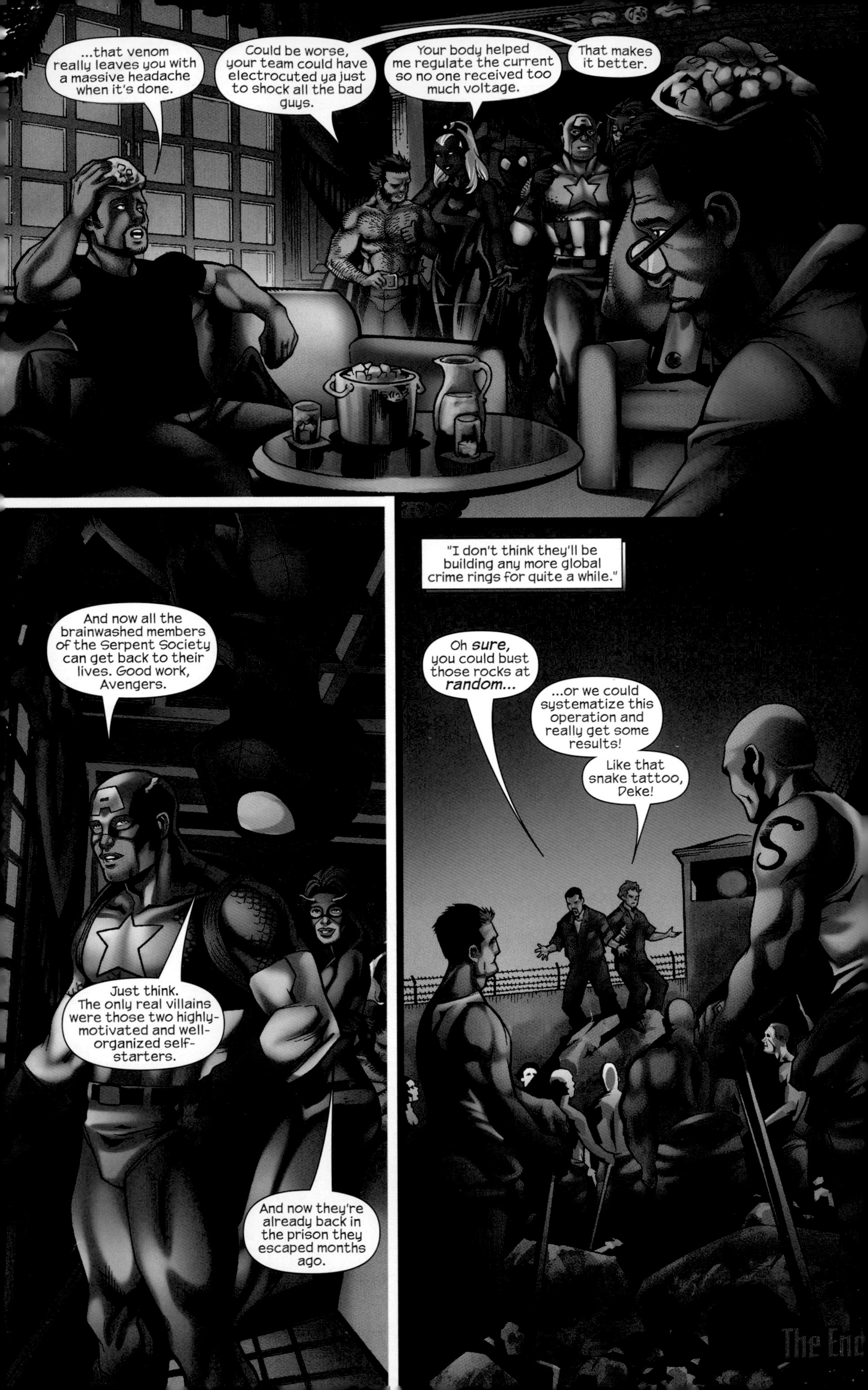

...that venom really leaves you with a massive headache when it's done.
Could be worse, your team could have electrocuted ya just to shock all the bad guys.
Your body helped me regulate the current so no one received too much voltage.
That makes it better.
And now all the brainwashed members of the Serpent Society can get back to their lives. Good work, Avengers.
Just think. The only real villains were those two highly-motivated and well-organized self-starters.
And now they're already back in the prison they escaped months ago.
"I don't think they'll be building any more global crime rings for quite a while."
Oh *sure,* you could bust those rocks at *random...*
...or we could systematize this operation and really get some results!
Like that snake tattoo, Deke!